INDIA

JENNY VAUGHAN

A⁺

Smart Apple Media

EMERGING NATIONS

INDIA

A+
Smart Apple Media

Published by Smart Apple Media, an imprint of Black Rabbit Books
P.O. Box 3263, Mankato, Minnesota 56002
www.blackrabbitbooks.com

Published by arrangement with the Watts Publishing Group LTD, London.

Cataloging-in-Publication Data is available from the Library of Congress
ISBN 978-1-59920-986-9 (library binding)
ISBN 978-1-62588-602-6 (eBook)

Series Editor: Julia Bird
Series Advisor: Emma Epsley, geography teacher and consultant
Series Design: sprout.uk.com

Photo credits:
AF Archive/Alamy: 37tl. AJP/Shutterstock: front cover t. Alamy Celebrity/Alamy: 37tr. arindambanerjee/Shutterstock: 34t.Ajay Bhaskar/Dreamstime 28. Oleg D/Shutterstock: 20.Dario Diament/Shutterstock: 37b. Excel Media/Rex Features: 13t. Kevin Fletcher/Dreamstime: 38.f9photos/Shutterstock: 43b.Christopher Furlong/Getty Images: 39t. Anna Furman/ Shutterstock: 39b. Gauravmasand/Dreamstime: 21b. gopixgo/Shutterstock: 6. Nick Gray/Wikimedia Commons: 10. Jorg Hackemann/Shutterstock: 26. Nick Hanna/Alamy: 29b. Andrew Holbrooke/Corbis: 21t.Jaguar PS/Shutterstock: 36. Maurice Joseph/Almay: 27. Lebrecht Music & Arts/Alamy: 35. LiteChoices/Shutterstock: 13b. Kistryn Malgorzata /Shutterstock: 19b. Matt McInnis/Dreamstime: 17t. Vladimir Meinik/Shutterstock: 9t. Julia Milberger/istockphoto: 30b. Nice prospects-Prime/ Alamy: 29b. OPIS Zagreb/Shutterstock: 30t. Christine Osborne Pictures/Alamy: 16. Pietrach/Dreamstime: 11t. Plus Lee/ Shutterstock: 17b. Paul Prescott/Shutterstock: 22, 31. Project1photography/Dreamstime: 11c. Jean-Baptiste Rabouan/Alamy: 19t. Daniel Rao/istockphoto: 24. Daniel J. Rao/Shutterstock: 25. Fredrik Renander/Alamy: 23. Jeremy Richards/Shutter-stock: 33. Samrat35/Dreamstime: 15t, 15b, 40. Sapsiwai/Shutterstock: 11b. Sipa Press/Rex Features: 12. Nickolay Stanev/ Shutterstock: front cover b, 8. Pavel Svobova/Shutterstock: 18. Pal Teravagimov/Shutterstock: 32. Aleksandaar Todorovic/ Shutterstock: 21c. View Pictures/UIG/Getty Images: 34b. Ian Walker/Dreamstime: 7b. World History Archive/Alamy: 9b. Zeber/Shutterstock: 14, 42. Artur Zebrowski/Dreamstime: 41t.

Every attempt has been made to clear copyright. Should there be any inadvertent omission please apply to the publisher for rectification.

Printed in the United States by CG Book Printers
North Mankato, Minnesota

PO 1721
3-2015

987654321

EMERGING NATIONS

INDIA

CONTENTS

CHAPTER 1

INTRODUCING INDIA
LAND OF CONTRASTS

India is the seventh largest country in the world. It covers 1.2 square million acres (3 million sq km) of south Asia and is a land of huge contrasts. The world's highest mountain range, the Himalayas, lies in the far north. In the south, the flat, fertile Indo-Gangetic Plain stretches from Pakistan in the west to Bangladesh in the east. The plain is made up largely of the Ganga (or Ganges) River basin. The Great Indian (or Thar) Desert forms a southern extension of the plain that stretches into Pakistan. Peninsular India juts out into the Indian Ocean and has a landscape of mountain ranges and hills.

The town of Darjiling (formerly Darjeeling) is in the Himalayas. The highest mountain in India, Kanchenjunga, can be seen in the background.

CLIMATE

India's climate varies from region to region. The mountainous north has freezing winters, while the Thar desert is very dry and the tropical south is lush and wet. India is described as having a monsoon climate, which means the seasons depend on the direction of the wind. From mid-June to early October, winds from the Indian Ocean carry moisture across India and bring rain. Between November and February, dry winds blow in from the interior of Asia. From March to June, and in October, there is little wind.

A CHANGING COUNTRY

The population of India is growing rapidly. It reached 1.2 billion in 2012. By contrast, when India achieved independence from colonial rule in 1947, the population was just 350 million. Once poor and undeveloped, India has been one of the fastest-growing economies in the world. Since the 1990s, it produces more goods and services every year. However, while some people have become very wealthy, poverty remains a great problem. An estimated quarter of the population live on less than $.67 a day.

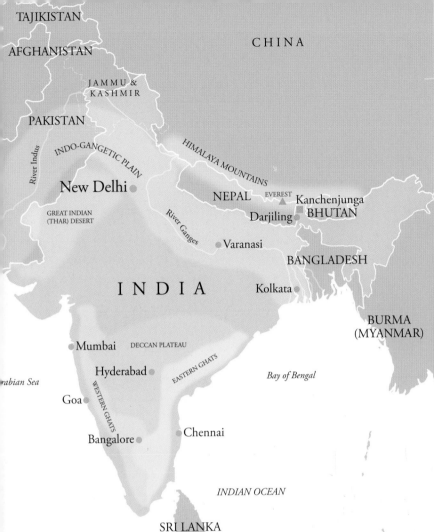

POPULATION GROWTH (2000–2012)

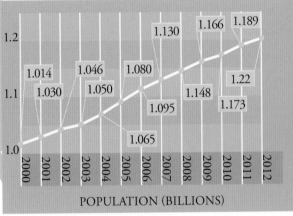

1.2

1.014
1.030

1.046
1.050

1.080

1.130

1.166

1.189

1.1

1.095

1.148

1.22

1.065

1.173

1.0

2000 2001 2002 2003 2004 2005 2006 2007 2008 2009 2010 2011 2012

POPULATION (BILLIONS)

NEW AND OLD

Rapid development has brought better schools and medical care for many; but it also has resulted in pollution, overcrowding, and great inequalities between people. However, the traditional values of Indian family life and religion remain important.

India's population growth is mostly taking place in its cities, which are growing by about 1.1 percent each year.

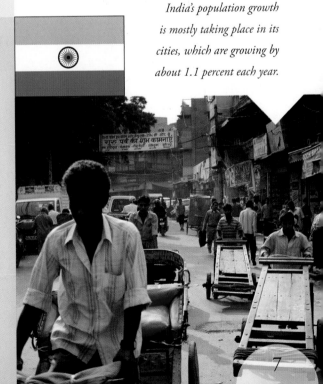

SPOTLIGHT ON INDIA

AREA: 1.3 million square miles (3.3 million sq km) • POPULATION: approx 1.2 billion • CAPITAL: New Delhi • LARGEST CITIES: Mumbai: 20.5 million; New Delhi: 22 million • LONGEST RIVER: The Ganga 1,560 miles (2,510 km) • HIGHEST MOUNTAIN: Kanchenjunga 28,170 feet (8,585 m) • MAIN LANGUAGES: Hindi 41%, Bengali 8.1%, Telugu 7.2%, Marathi 7%, Tamil 5.9%, Urdu 5% • MAIN RELIGIONS: Hindu 80.5%, Muslim 13.4%, Christian 2.3%, Sikh 1.9% • NATURAL RESOURCES: petroleum, coal, natural gas, iron ore, copper, bauxite, ceramic clays, diamonds

PAST INTO PRESENT

ANCIENT INDIA

The first cities on the Indian subcontinent grew over 4,000 years ago in present-day Pakistan. India's main religion—now called Hinduism—developed about 3,000 years ago and possibly after settlers arrived from Central Asia.

FOREIGN INVADERS

Approximately between 320 and 1000 AD, after centuries of being small kingdoms, larger Indian empires grew. In 1526, Muslim invaders set up the Mughal Empire in India. The British traded with the Mughals through the privately owned East India Company. Eventually this became more powerful than the Mughals, and even had its own army. In 1857, Indian soldiers in this army rebelled. Following this, the British government took direct control of India, although Indians continued to campaign for independence. From 1885, this struggle was led by the Indian National Congress, which is still a major political party today.

INDEPENDENCE AND AFTERWARD

India won independence in 1947 with the partition of the country into predominantly Hindu India and the largely Muslim Pakistan. As people from both communities fled across the new borders, violence left approximately a million people dead. Until 1972, Pakistan was divided into two parts: West Pakistan and East Pakistan with India located between them. In 1972, following a war between India and both parts of Pakistan, East Pakistan became independent Bangladesh—with India's support. West Pakistan simply remained Pakistan.

The Presidential House in New Delhi, designed by British architect Edwin Landseer Lutyens, shows the British legacy in India.

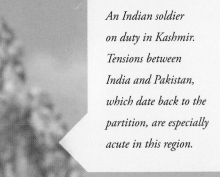

An Indian soldier on duty in Kashmir. Tensions between India and Pakistan, which date back to the partition, are especially acute in this region.

TENSIONS

Although they live in one of the world's fastest-growing economies, many Indians remain poor. This wealth gap dates partly from British rule when development was designed more to make money for the rulers than the mass of the people. Many Indians also blame governments since independence for mismanaging the economy. Poverty, and tensions between Hindus and Muslims, have made Indian politics volatile. Occasional outbreaks of rioting and violence occur. Relations between India and Pakistan are strained. War has broken out several times—mostly over the region of Kashmir, which is claimed by both countries. This is especially dangerous as both countries are now nuclear powers.

MAHATMA GANDHI

PEACEFUL PROTESTOR

Mahatma Gandhi is the most famous campaigner for Indian independence. Born in 1869 in Gujarat, Gandhi trained as a lawyer in London. As leader of the Indian National Congress, he led the campaign for independence and was imprisoned as a dangerous rebel although he always rejected violence. Gandhi opposed the partition of India and was assassinated by a Hindu extremist in 1948. Gandhi's belief in the importance of nonviolent protest lives on today, and he is honored by peace movements all over the world.

Mumbai is the capital of the Indian state of Maharashtra. Originally called Bombay, it was an island with that name off India's west coast. In 1995, the Maharashtra state government officially changed Bombay's name to Mumbai (a name some local people had always used), after a Hindu goddess, Mumba, who is especially important to the city. Renaming the city was part of a move throughout India to change place names associated with British rule. Today, Mumbai is India's wealthiest and most populous city.

MUMBAI IN HISTORY

The area around Mumbai has been settled for thousands of years and was an important port as long ago as 1000 BC. After a brief under Portuguese rule, the powerful British East India Company established control over the city. In the 1850s, cotton-spinning and weaving mills were set up. Trade flourished, especially during the US Civil War when no cotton was exported from the United States and Mumbai became wealthy.

MUMBAI TODAY

Textiles are still important, but Mumbai is a center for many industries. These include metals, electronics, chemicals, and making cars. It is also the home of Bollywood—India's film hub (see page 36) and India's financial center.

CROWDED CITY

Being on an island, Mumbai has always been densely populated. By the end of the 19th century, it was already overcrowded.

In the 1950s, it spread northward after a causeway was built to a neighboring island, Salsette. Today, the Mumbai Metropolitan Region takes in the city of Mumbai and a number of satellite towns. It is one of the world's most heavily populated cities with more than 20 million inhabitants—up from approximately 12 million in 1991. Mumbai's population density is about 30,000 people per .4 square miles (1 sq km)—believed to be the highest in the world.

The Haji Ali Dargah is a tomb and mosque. This famous Mumbai landmark is visited by people of all religions. It is linked to the city by a road that can only be reached at low tide.

People shop at a Mumbai street market. Mumbai has modern shops and supermarkets, but many people prefer to buy food from open-air markets.

Chowpatty Beach, Mumbai. Mumbai has a number of beaches. This is its best known and often one of the most crowded.

A group of film extras pose on the set of an Indian-made movie. Mumbai is a center for movie making and is often called Bollywood—a mix of Bombay and Hollywood.

11

CHAPTER 2:
LIVING IN INDIA
A DIVIDED DEMOCRACY

RIGHT TO VOTE

With 1.2 billion inhabitants, India has 17 percent of the world's population. One out of six people on Earth lives in India. Only China has more people. But India is a democracy and the world's largest. Politicians are voted in during elections to run India and its 28 states. The Indian National Congress is the oldest political party. Its main rival, the BJP, is linked to the Hindu religion. As many as 700 million Indians have the right to vote if they are over the age of 18 and not mentally challenged or a criminal.

Indian voters lined up to vote in the 2009 general election. With 714 million eligible voters, 828,804 polling stations were needed.

POWERHOUSE

India has an elected president, but the real power lies with the prime minister, who is the leader of whichever party has the most members of parliament in the Lok Sabha (House of the People). This is one of two houses of parliament. The other is the Rajya Sabha (Council of States) whose members are elected by parliaments in each state.

LANGUAGE

Communication is vital to politics and the economy, but this is made difficult by the fact that India has hundreds of tribal and national groups in India. Each has their own languages, dialects, and cultures. To make communication easier, Hindi has been made a national language. English, a second official language, is widely spoken in business.

UNEQUAL WEALTH

Although India is home to some of the world's richest people, an estimated one in four people in India is hungry. Poverty is unevenly spread. In the northern state of Bihar in 2010, for example, approximately 53.5 percent of people lived in poverty. In the state of Jammu and Kashmir, it was just over 9 percent. This is partly because some areas have better resources than others. Also, both foreign and domestic investment favors some parts of India more than others. Deep divisions between rich and poor can encourage resentment, crime, and violence.

Children often have to contribute to family income. This girl is collecting cotton waste from a factory to sell for a small price.

WHAT COUNTS AS POOR?

The World Bank measures absolute poverty as less than $1.25 (79p) per day per person to live on. Using this, 2010 poverty levels were estimated as:

- Bangladesh: 43.3% • India: 32.7% • Pakistan: 21%
- China: 13.1% • Mexico: 1.2% (2009)
- Romania: 0.4% (2009)

(No countries in North America or Western Europe had such high levels.)

India's official 2012 measure of poverty is 32 rupees ($.54) a day in cities and 26 rupees ($.44) a day in villages. This puts numbers living in poverty at under 30 percent. But critics say India's measure is too low, and that by using more widely accepted measures of $1.25 or $2 a day, the figures would be much higher—possibly as high as 50 percent.

COMMUNICATIONS

Good communications and transportation links are vital in a country as large as India and are all the more important as India grows into a world economic power.

ON THE ROAD

Approximately half of all roads—about 950,000 miles (1,530,000 km)—have hard surfaces. The remainder are unpaved and are easily damaged in poor weather. However, car ownership in India is growing fast. In 2000, fewer than 0.5 percent of Indians owned a car. Some estimates put this at nearly 5 percent in 2011.

AIR AND RAIL LINKS

For millions, traditional forms of transportation, such as hand-drawn rickshaws and bullock carts, are all that is available. Even public transportation is a problem in isolated villages. A bus stop may be several hours' walk away. By contrast, better-off people can use air travel. India's domestic passenger numbers reached about 60.7 million in 2011—up 74 percent from 2006 levels. Rail is important to India's economy. With around 40,000 miles (65,000 km) of railways, the trains can carry around 7 billion passengers a year and over a billion tons of freight.

Auto-rickshaws or "tuk-tuks" are a common sight on India's roads. These three-seater vehicles are very economical to run.

जय श्री श्याम

KEEPING IN TOUCH

In a rural area of Madhya Pradesh state, in central India, a man talks on a cell phone. These are very popular in areas where there are not enough landlines.

India's first telegraph systems were set up in the 1850s. Landline telephones came into use in the 1880s. As in many developing countries, cell telephones, which do not need expensive wiring, are often more practical. The first cell phones were used in India in the 1990s. Today, India has about a billion subscribers. The Internet is used widely in business. Many homes also have access. People who do not have the Internet at home use Internet cafés.

India's beautiful beaches attract tourists from all over the world.

TOURISM

Mumbai is one of the most important of India's seaports where goods are imported and exported. It also handles more than half of India's international flights. Many of these flights bring tourists—around 6 million each year, mostly from the U.S. and Europe. In 2010, tourism contributed $14 billion to India's GDP—over 6 percent of the total. Tourism can help to support heritage sites, such as ancient temples and wildlife parks, which might otherwise be overlooked in a rush for development. But tourism has its downside: it can damage the environment, use up scarce land and water resources, and have a distorting effect on local culture as people adapt traditional art and crafts to please visitors.

LIVING STANDARDS

Like everything else in India, housing differs greatly due to the differences between the rich and the poor.

HEALTHCARE

India does have some world-class private hospitals. People from richer countries may choose to attend them for treatment, which is often cheaper than in the West. The poor use state-run clinics and programs for vaccinating children against dangerous diseases. Charities run clinics in the slums and rural areas. But these are not sufficient for India's booming population, and paying for private care—which many Indians must do—can push families into poverty.

A rural vaccination clinic in Goa, India. Indian parents are encouraged to have their babies immunized against a range of diseases, including polio, diphtheria, and measles.

ELECTRICITY

In 2003, the Indian government set a goal to provide "power for all" by 2012, but as many as 70,000 villages still do not have electricity. Even in cities, electricity supplies are not reliable. The country's rapid development puts a great strain on its electricity supply network. As a result, frequent power cuts occur. In July 2012, half the country went without electricity. Public transportation and factories came to a standstill. The system needs modernizing and India needs new power stations. But it is not always easy for people to agree to these being built—especially when it involves damming rivers for hydroelectric power. Paying for it is another issue. Despite its growing wealth, the Indian government has little money to spend. Many people are too poor to pay much—if any—tax.

Millions of Indians do not have access to enough clean drinking water. For example, approximately 100,000 people live in one slum outside Delhi and share just one tap, which is turned on three times a day. One of the biggest dangers to health is from water polluted with human or animal waste. Only 15 percent of people in rural areas have access to a toilet. In city slums, many ditches are open sewers running between the houses.

There are encouraging signs, however. In 1990, approximately 33 percent of Indians had no access to safe drinking water. By 2008, this was down to 17 percent. In 1990, 75 percent of people in India did not have access to hygienic toilets. That was reduced to 58 percent by 2008.

An Indian mother and daughter fetch water at the rural community well in Khuri, a village in Rajasthan.

EDUCATION

Children in Darjiling, in northern India, are on their way home from school. In rural areas, children may have to walk several miles (km) to and from school.

Good education is essential for any country that wants to compete in the modern world. Providing this is one of greatest challenges facing India.

GOING TO SCHOOL

In 2009, India made education free and compulsory for all children from 6 to 14. However, not every child gets to go to school. Estimates of those not enrolled in school vary widely—between 5 and 20 percent. It is accepted that enrolled pupils are often absent. In some communities, children may be expected to work instead of study. In the case of girls, they are expected to help at home. In rural areas, schools are too far away for children to reach. By secondary level, estimates of children attending school range from 60 percent down to 40 percent.

AROUND INDIA

Education levels between states vary. As with fighting poverty, Kerala, in the south, does well. It has 90 percent literacy, compared with 64 percent in Bihar. Everywhere, girls fare worse than boys in education. In more traditional households, girls are held back in education, kept at home, and encouraged to marry early.

FOREIGN CAMPUSES

Several foreign universities have set up campuses in India to attract students with the option of studying at home. These include U.K. universities Leeds Metropolitan in Bhopal and Lancaster, which runs management courses in Delhi. U.S. universities include Virginia Tech, which opened a research center in Tamil Nadu in 2013.

BRAIN DRAIN

One problem India faces is keeping its most highly qualified people. Many graduates leave for the United States, Europe, and Australia for better career opportunities and higher wages. For example, a senior scientist in an Indian university might earn $33,565 a year—but can earn four or five times that in the United States.

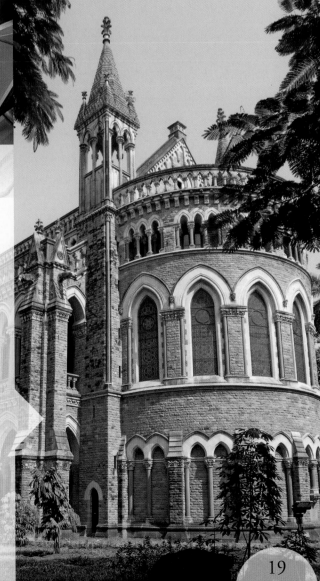

UNIVERSITY AND COLLEGE

India has high-quality universities and colleges, such as the University of Mumbai, whose history goes back over 100 years. These higher level schools have played an important part in educating India's politicians, scientists, and business people over the years. The Indian government believes that higher education must expand if India's economy is to go on growing. Approximately 12 percent of young Indians attend universities, and plans are in progress to increase this to 30 percent. Hundreds of new universities and colleges are being set up—some by overseas universities that are building campuses in India (see panel).

A computer class is held at Mayo College, Ajmer, in Rajasthan. This private school was founded in 1870 by the British Viceroy (ruler) of India, Lord Mayo, for the sons of Indian princes.

The University of Mumbai, founded in 1857, is one of India's oldest and most important universities.

Life in Mumbai presents many of the same advantages and problems as the rest of India. These play out against the backdrop of a busy, heavily populated, developing city.

HIGH-RISE VS. SLUMS

A 27-story house belonging to a wealthy Indian businessman stands out against Mumbai's skyline. It is not the only luxurious home in Mumbai, as the city is home to many incredibly rich people. Yet, by contrast, more than 60 percent of Mumbai's inhabitants live on only a few hundred dollars a year, in crowded slums without clean drinking water or proper sanitation.

A MIDDLE CLASS

Like many other Indian cities, Mumbai has a growing middle class that earns less than those in similar jobs in Europe and the United States, but still may be able to afford luxury items such as televisions. Some estimate that as many as 50 million Indians are part of this class. If the Indian economy continues to expand at its current rate, it could grow by as much as ten times within the next ten years.

Living space is at a premium in Mumbai, so rents are high. Many middle-class families still live in aging blocks called "chawls." These are often overcrowded and in need of repair, but it gives extended family members a chance to live close to each other at low rents.

MOVING MILLIONS

Like many Indians, few Mumbaikars (Mumbai people) own cars, but this number is increasing fast, as approximately 450 new vehicles are registered every day. One consequence is polluted air from traffic fumes. But most people (approximately 90 percent) rely on public transportation. The local railway transports about 7 million commuters a day.

Others use buses. Like the trains and the roads themselves, the buses are incredibly crowded. Richer travelers may be able to travel by motorized rickshaws. Ferries operate between the islands. A metro system is also being built to help relieve the crowds on the roads and trains.

Yet, India remains a land where old and new live side by side. It is no surprise to see hand-drawn rickshaws and bullock carts are still commonplace on Mumbai's crowded streets.

Tuk-tuks in Mumbai add to the pollution in the city's air. Recently, less polluting engines have been developed to help reduce this problem.

Rush hour on Mumbai's busy commuter trains. Mumbai's suburban train network transports more than 7 million passengers every day.

Almost in the center of the city, Dharavi is a huge Mumbai slum. Over half a million people live there, mostly in illegal settlements with very poor sanitation.

This luxurious apartment building is on Mumbai's exclusive Marine Drive, near Chowpatty Beach. Only the very rich can afford to live in buildings like these.

CHAPTER 3:
INDIA AT WORK
ECONOMIC POWERHOUSE

FULL SPEED AHEAD

India's GDP (Gross Domestic Product—the value of everything it produces) has grown at an average of 7 percent since 1997. By contrast, in the United States and Europe, GDP has barely grown at all. However, India's growth has begun to slow down.

PAST AND PRESENT

In the past, India's industry was mostly small scale, such as making pots for local use. Industries still exist, but others have become far more important. Textiles (cloth and clothing) make more than one-quarter of India's income from exports. India is the second largest textile producer after China. Major retailers, such as Gucci, Gap, and Calvin Klein, use Indian factories. Unfortunately, this industry has a poor reputation all over the world and relies on sweatshops. The workers put in long hours for low wages in overcrowded conditions. The best importers inspect the factories regularly to make sure conditions are acceptable.

SWEATSHOPS

India is accused of being the world's sweatshop capital. Children as young as five are often employed in the textile industry. In 2012, the Indian government gave its support to a plan to make employing anyone under 14 a crime and punishable by three years in prison.

Men at work in a textile factory. This industry provides a great boost to India's exports, but people may work long hours for little pay.

TECHNOLOGICAL REVOLUTION

In the 1990s, the Indian government decided to prioritize the growth of its software industry. To make up for India's often unreliable telephone system, the government invested in high-quality satellite communications. In south India, Bangalore (also called Bengaluru) became the main center of the industry. It was already a base for electronic companies and research institutions for India's military. The industry soon took off. Today, many multinational electronics companies have Indian design and development centers. Successful Indian companies, such as Infosys and Wipro Ltd, have grown and developed alongside huge software multinationals such as Microsoft.

OTHER INDUSTRIES

Tata Motors, a world-leading motor manufacturer, has its head office in Mumbai and factories throughout India. It was set up after World War II to make commercial vehicles, and began making passenger cars in the 1990s, including the Tata Nano, an inexpensive car for the home market. Tata has expanded over the years to take in foreign companies, such as Jaguar LandRover from the UK.

CALLING INDIA

Over the past 10 years, India has become a successful base for call centers. Many international companies, such as banks and mobile phone companies, looked to cut costs by employing Indian workers to staff their help desks. However, this once booming industry is now on the wane. Large global businesses, such as the huge banking group Santander, relocated their call centers to their countries of origin to improve customer service. Other countries, such as the Philippines, are also beginning to emerge as cheaper call-center hubs.

These two young women are Information Technology workers in Bangalore. About a third of India's IT professionals work in Bangalore.

AGRICULTURE

Despite its expanding industrial sector, India is still at heart a rural country. At least half of all workers are involved in farming. Agriculture makes up about a fifth of India's GDP.

SMALL FARMS

Women picking tea on a plantation. India produces about 30 percent of the world's tea, employing more than 2 million people.

Indians spend 25 percent of their income on food. Most food comes from smallscale subsistence farms. Farmers grow food for their families and a little extra to sell. Crops include vegetables, such as rice and corn; fruit, such as bananas and mangoes; and staples, such as rice and wheat.

CHANGING WAYS

Until recently, only a few crops, such as tea, coffee, and cotton, were major exports. Now, other crops are exported. In Punjab, for example, large amounts of wheat are grown to be sold internationally. In 2010, India produced 88 million tons (80 t) of wheat, making it the world's third largest producer (after China and the European Union) and the seventh largest exporter.

LIVESTOCK

Cattle are sacred to Hindus. Many people keep just a few cows. There are few large herds, but collectively, they amount to 2 million animals—15 percent of all the cattle in the world. They are kept for milk, rather than meat. Poultry is also raised on small farms for eggs and meat.

FISHING

About 3.5 million people live in villages along the Indian coastline and earn a living from fishing. Millions more depend on the industry. But it is under threat. Larger, powered craft can take over small boats and cause a danger of over-fishing. This could lead to the collapse of fish stocks and make it impossible for fishing communities to survive. Many believe it is vital that the Indian government finds a way to prevent this from happening.

Inland, the government encourages fish-farming in areas such as West Bengal, where there is plenty of fresh water. About 3.9 million tons (3.5 million t) of fish are harvested in inland India—more than half of it now from farms. In the future, India could expand this three times over.

Fishing off the Malabar coast in southwestern India. Today, small traditional fishing boats are facing competition from large mechanized ships.

EMPLOYMENT IN INDIA

India's total workforce is about 478 million. Many people (perhaps as many as 90 percent) work in the "informal" sector—that is, outside of government control. This makes it difficult to know how many people are employed in different ways, but estimates are:

agriculture 52% • services 34% • industry 14%

25

FARMING CHALLENGES

Subsistence farming is more challenging than large-scale agriculture. With one stroke of bad luck, such as a flood or drought, or an outbreak of illness among the livestock, a family or whole community can go hungry.

THE "GREEN REVOLUTION"

Indian farmers tackle the insecurities they face by adopting more modern farming methods. Many now buy and plant high-yielding seeds instead of using grain they have saved from previous years. They also apply chemical fertilizers, as well as animal dung, to enrich soil. Ox-drawn plows are giving way to tractors. This change in farming, which began in the 1960s, is called "the Green Revolution" and has massively increased food production.

THE DOWNSIDE

New technology is not always good news. Older seed varieties and traditional crops are more resistant to drought and do not cost much to grow. The high price of new seeds and artificial fertilizers can lead farmers into debt. Many thousands of farmers have been forced to leave the countryside for the cities to make money.

LAND RIGHTS

Many rural people are Adivasi, descendents of the earliest people to live in India. They may always have lived in an area, but it is hard to prove their right to be there. Big projects, such as mines and reservoirs, may try to throw them off the land. In 2012, protests forced the Indian government to promise more legal rights and better compensation to people displaced by such projects.

Corn is being transported in Rajasthan, northwest India. Getting food from farms to the people who need it is often a problem, and too often, crops go to waste.

Adivasi women at a market in Orissa, eastern India.

OUR LAND!

Chembakolli village is in the Nilgiri Hills in Tamil Nadu. The people there are Adivasi. In 1988, the people of the Nilgiri Hills joined a campaign to get traditionally held land back. In 1990, they succeeded. Today, many Chembakolli people are still poor. However, they live in concrete houses with good roofs, and the children can go to school. They have their own tea plantation and sell tea all over the world.

27

Indians call Mumbai "the land of opportunities." Its history as a trading center goes back as far as the 1600s when it exported textiles, jewelery, cotton, and rice.

MODERN MUMBAI

Mumbai is the commercial capital of India and its center of finance and banking. It is one of the world's top 10 centers of commerce and contributes about a quarter of India's industrial output. Many large foreign companies have offices in Mumbai, including the communications and technology giant Siemens.

Other industries include software companies, pharmaceutical manufacturers, and heavy industry, such as making products of steel and rubber. The long tradition of textile and garment manufacture still survives. All this offers work to millions. Some work in factories and offices, but many others work in the informal sector.

INFORMAL WORK

The informal sector is made up of people who have little contact with the government. They do not pay tax and are often self-employed. They may make clothing or leather goods, drive rickshaws, or find casual work as laborers. Often, they support families who live far away in the villages. Huge amounts of money can be made in these smaller areas of industry. Some estimate that the annual economic output of the sprawling Dharavi slum could be as much as $1 billion. Many Dharavi residents have little to show for it, although things are beginning to slowly improve. This is largely due to many years of campaigning among the residents of the slum and people working with them.

High-rise buildings are a way to provide homes for the millions who live in Mumbai. These luxury flats are too expensive for most people.

Every day in Mumbai, about 5,000 deliverymen carry 175,000 "tiffin tins" (containers of lunches) to factories and offices.

The Mumbai head office of the State Bank of India is just one of the major banks in Mumbai.

These pots are made in the Dharavi slum. They are sold for everyday use all over India.

ENVIRONMENTAL COSTS

India's development has brought jobs and wealth to many, but it comes at a cost for the environment.

WATER SHORTAGE

Modern farming methods help provide food for India's growing population, but this requires huge amounts of water. In the Punjab region, so much water is used to grow wheat and rice that the aquifer (underground water) levels are dropping and affecting vital supplies. Mining and quarrying provide important fuel and building materials, but drain water away. Bridges and dams block rivers. The need for water and hydroelectric power stations has led to more and more dams being built. These are controversial, as land where people once lived and farmed is now flooded.

SOIL

Deforestation is a major problem. Often, it is the result of logging—trees being chopped down for timber. Land is also cleared for farming. Poor farming methods, which include using too much chemical fertilizer, can damage the soil, leaving it bare. As it washes away, rivers become clogged and the danger of floods increases. Wind can blow soil away, creating deserts and ruining crops. About half of India's land surface is affected by soil loss. For India to continue to develop, it is important to educate farmers to look after the soil. A number of government initiatives are trying to help farmers manage the land better. Laws have been passed against illegal logging.

The Tehri Dam reservoir is in northern India. Although it can produce massive amounts of power and water, the dam has resulted in local people losing their land and livelihoods.

When forests are cut down, wildlife and people who depend on forest plants suffer. The soil may also be washed away and no longer good for food production.

WATER POLLUTION

India's rivers are often polluted with sewage as well as chemicals from farms and factories. The River Ganga, which is sacred to the Hindu religion, is particularly badly affected. It flows for over 1,500 miles (2,500 km), supplying water to 400 million people. Two-thirds of the untreated sewage and industrial waste from towns and cities along its banks flows into the river. The Indian government has had an action plan since the 1980s to clean up the Ganga. In 2010, the plan's second phase was rolled out. Billions of dollars are to be spent tackling pollution and using the sewage to produce biogas to generate electricity.

AIR

India's rapid development has resulted in a big increase in its greenhouse gas emissions, the gases believed to be responsible for climate change. India's greenhouse gas emissions rose by an estimated 58 percent between 1994 and 2007, making India the fourth largest producer of greenhouse gases after China, the United States, and the European Union. In some cities, such as Delhi, "green taxes" are being considered to discourage drivers, while public transportation and bicycle lanes are being improved. This should help reduce both greenhouse gases and air pollution.

Smog hangs over the city of Delhi. Scientists warn that the level of pollution in Delhi is dangerous to people's health.

CHAPTER 4:
CHANGING CULTURE
RELIGION AND CASTE

For most Indians, religion is an important part of their lives, whichever faith they follow.

THREAT TO TRADITION

Hinduism is the religion of the largest number of Indians. For devout Hindus, who reject material wealth, rapid development can seem alarming. The fact that India is officially a secular (nonreligious) state is only partly accepted by traditionalists. Many view the growing modernization of everyday life—especially among women (see page 41)—as a threat to long-held beliefs and values.

CASTE

The caste system is a social structure linked to Hinduism. People are born into their caste. This affects every part of their lives— where they live, who they marry, what jobs they do, and more.

Discrimination on the grounds of caste is illegal, but it still happens. It is beginning to break down as India develops, but it is not fast enough for the "dalits" (once known as "untouchables")—the 20 percent of Indians at the bottom of the caste system. They have few opportunities and have the lowest-paying jobs. Dalits make up about 90 percent of India's poor, who see little of the positive side of Indian development.

ISLAM

Even after independence, when millions fled into Pakistan for safety, many Muslims remained in India. They now make up approximately 13.5 percent of the population. Muslims often suffer discrimination in today's India. A high proportion (nearly a quarter in cities) are poor and, like the dalits, are often excluded from India's race to development.

Hindu pilgrims bathe in the River Ganga in the holy city of Varanasi in northern India. Devout Hindus hope to visit the city at least once in a lifetime.

32

Dalit children stitch soccer balls. Dalits have "impure" jobs, such as working with leather. It is considered to be unclean due to its association with killing cows, butchery, and waste.

Indian Muslims at prayer at the Jama Masjid, which is the most important mosque in Old Delhi.

RIVALRY

Rivalry between the Muslims and Hindus is centuries old, and dates from the earliest Mughal invasions. The bloodshed at partition stemmed from this rivalry, and made it worse. Both religions have fundamentalist wings, which can inflame violence between different communities. One of the worst events in memory took place in 1992. Riots all over India left more than 2,000 people dead after militant Hindus destroyed a mosque in Ayodhya, Uttar Pradesh. Many other similar events have occurred since, bringing instability to the country and dividing the population.

FAMILY TIES

For Indians of all religions, family is deeply important. It means that people believe family members must care for each other and share their wealth. But it can also lead to nepotism—unfairly favoring family members in employment and other opportunities. This can be a threat to development as it may exclude talented people from the economy.

THE ARTS

In the past, Indian art was mainly linked to religion. India's beautiful temples, mosques, and other religious monuments attract millions of visitors every year. India's literature, too, was often rooted in religion.

ARCHITECTURE

By contrast, today's India has plenty of fine modern architecture. Much of it reflects India's role as a rapidly developing and modern country. These include public buildings, airport terminals, and innovative office buildings—such as the GMS Grande Palladium in Mumbai. However, experts warn against building too much, too fast. India's infrastructure—its roads and power supply—need to be improved if modern construction is to be a success. Some critics say it is as important to find ways to build appropriate, affordable housing in India's crowded cities. Approximately 19 million people still need adequate homes.

GMS Grande Palladium is in Mumbai. This new office block was designed by Malik Architecture—one of the country's top firms of architects.

A scene from the Ramayana is acted out at a theater in Hyderabad.

THE WRITTEN WORD

Ancient Hindu epics, the *Ramayana*, *Mahabharata*, and *Bhagavad Gita* were written 2,500 years ago. These tell the stories of ancient gods and heroes. They are still read and made into films, plays, and poetry. But in India today, much new literature is written in English and is available to readers all over the world. This includes the work of writers such as novelists Salman Rushdie, Anita Desai, and Arundhati Roy. These writers have played an important part in introducing modern India to the rest of the world, as Indian drama is gradually finding its way onto the stages of Europe and the United States.

Vasu Dixit, of Indian band Swarathma, performed at the 2010 Larmer Tree Festival in the UK. Swarathma is a band based in Bangalore that combines folk tunes and Western sounds.

MUSIC

As with most Indian art, music has a long history and was first played in temples and palaces. Classical Indian music and traditional instruments such as the sitar are played today. But like so much in India, ancient traditions are now often combined with modern influences to create a unique mix that includes rock and pop, for example, by adding a modern beat to traditional Hindi songs.

AN INDIAN ARTIST

Many world-class modern artists and sculptors live and work in India today. Atul Dodiya (born 1959) was born and lives in Mumbai and studied at the city's Sir Jamsetjee Jeejebhoy School of Art (Sir JJ School of Art). His work includes paintings and installations that are often inspired by Mumbai's most famous product— Bollywood films (see page 36).

Mumbai's media industry is huge. Many Indian radio and television stations are based there as well as national and local newspapers.

PRINT AND BROADCASTING

Like other cities, Mumbai has its own magazines and newspapers, as well as local editions of national papers, such as the *Times of India*. Mumbai has nine local radio stations, including those belonging to India's national public radio company, Akashvani. Also called All India Radio—it is one of the world's biggest broadcasters. Radio, which reaches nearly everyone, is especially important in a country where many people cannot read.

Approximately half of the households in Mumbai have a television. Most are served by one of the three main cable systems. Together, this brings over a hundred television channels to the city in a range of languages. Doordarshan, the national television broadcaster, has two free broadcast channels on air.

SPORTS AND THE MEDIA

Media plays an important part in India's favorite sport, cricket, which is a multi-million-dollar business. The television rights are controlled from Mumbai by the Board of Control for Cricket in India (BCCI)—the world's richest cricket governing body. Mumbai's own team—the Mumbai Indians—has an estimated 3 million fans worldwide.

BOLLYWOOD

Perhaps the best-known form of Indian media is its massive film industry, which is set to bring in approximately $25 billion in 2014. Bollywood produces hundreds of films each year. India as a whole produces more films than any other country in the world. These are exported all over the globe to wherever the worldwide Indian diaspora of 25 million people (see page 38) live. Many of the films involve music and dance.

Hrithik Roshan is one of the biggest Bollywood stars. He is pictured at the Cannes Film Festival with Uruguayan actress Bárbara Mori.

The 2008 hit film Slumdog Millionaire, set and filmed in Mumbai, brought Indian film to a worldwide audience.

A roadside fruit seller in Mumbai reads one of the city's many newspapers.

World-famous cricket player Sachin Tendulkar, at the IPL final between the Mumbai Indians and Chennai Super Kings.

CHAPTER 5:
THE CHANGING FACE OF INDIA
INDIA IN THE MODERN WORLD

India's role in the world is changing as its economy, people, and culture continue to make more and more of an impact.

THE DIASPORA

The Indian diaspora (people of Indian origin moving to other countries) is huge—around 25 million. Migration began during British rule. Many poor Indians were encouraged (or forced by extreme poverty) to travel to distant parts of the world. Once there, they were often bound by unfair contracts called "indentures" to remain, more or less, as slaves. As a result, Africa, the Caribbean, and many other places have longstanding communities of people of Indian origin. These communities grew as their families joined them.

NEW HOMES

In the 20th century, large numbers of Indians migrated to Britain, the United States, and Australia. With few opportunities in India, many took the opportunity to settle in wealthier parts of the world with wages that were much higher. The first arrivals were mostly men. Later, their families joined them, and new communities of people of Indian origin grew up.

People of Indian origin living in London celebrate Holi—the Hindu festival of colors.

BIG BUSINESS

India's 100 richest people have amassed around $250 billion among them. Many operate all over the world, such as Lakshmi Mittal, head of the world's largest steelmaking company, with businesses in more than 60 countries. Mittal, who is based in London, is the second richest Indian after Mumbai-based Mukesh Ambani, who has made a fortune in oil and gas. These wealthy businesses grew up in an India that is becoming 5 or 6 percent richer every year. Although this rate has been slowing down, it is still a huge contrast with the economies of Europe and the United States, where growth has been very limited. As India's economy expands, many European and American businesses are looking to India as a new market for their goods and services.

This sculpture was designed for the London 2012 Olympics by the Indian-born British sculptor, Anish Kapoor. It was mostly funded by ArcelorMittal, whose chairman is the Indian billionaire, Lakshmi Mittal.

TRADITIONAL BELIEFS

While India's business is booming and its scientists, writers, and other skilled people are making an impact in the world, India remains a land of ancient tradition. As India's people have settled in other parts of the world, they have brought with them ancient beliefs. These include their traditional Ayurvedic herbal medicine and stress-reducing techniques such as meditation and yoga—all of which have become popular in the West.

Yoga originated in India. It is now practiced throughout the world as a means of seeking inner peace.

WOMEN IN INDIA

A couple celebrates their marriage in Kolkota, West Bengal. Most Indians support the traditional belief that a marriage should be arranged by the couple's parents.

As India changes, the position of women in society reflects the divide between long-held tradition and modern development.

SUCCESS STORIES

Many Indian women have made remarkable achievements. A woman—Indira Gandhi—became prime minister in 1966. India has also had a woman president, Pratibha Devisingh Patil (2007–2012). Indian women have been successful in many other areas of work and industry. India has the largest number of professionally qualified women in the world, including more female doctors, scientists, and professors than the United States.

DOWRIES

In traditional Indian society, sons are valued more highly than daughters. A boy, it is believed, will support his parents one day. A girl will join another family on her marriage, and her in-laws may demand money or property on marriage (a dowry). Dowries were made illegal in the 1960s, but this has never been strictly enforced. The pressure of providing a dowry drives many families into debt—an estimated 80 percent of bank loans in India are used to finance dowry demands. Some brides have been murdered for their dowries by greedy in-laws.

GENDER IMBALANCE

At worst, families may opt to abort an unborn daughter rather than face poverty. An estimated 6 million unborn girls were aborted in India in the last 10 years. As a result, in 2011, for every 1,000 boys under the age of six, there were just 914 girls. If this gender imbalance continues, India will suffer as a generation of men will be unable to marry and have families. The Indian government is trying to change this by banning doctors from revealing a baby's sex and by subsidizing girls' higher education.

Education for girls still lags behind boys. Many pressure groups, as well as government policies, encourage parents to send their daughters to school.

SCHOOLING

Girls also suffer in education. They may leave school early or be kept at home so often that they fall behind. In 2010, the literacy level among girls was just under 75 percent, compared with nearly 87 percent of boys. However, attitudes are changing as people realize that educating girls benefits entire families in terms of health, education, and earning power. An Indian observation is "When you educate a woman, you educate a family."

ROLE OF WOMEN

Tensions still exist about the position of women. Modern Indian women who go out to work may be treated with hostility and even violence by traditionally minded people (men and women.) Some cling to the old belief that women should be treated as the property of their father or husbands.

A SHOCKING STORY

In December 2012, a young woman was raped and murdered on a bus in Delhi. Massive street demonstrations followed as Indians protested violence against women. They protested about the urgent need to solve the problem of overcoming traditional attitudes toward women that could allow men to think they could behave like this. Unless this happens, advocates say, India cannot call itself a modern country.

CHANGING TIMES

Since 2003, infant mortality in India has dropped from 60 per 1,000 births in 2003 to 44 in 2011, due to public education programs.

India certainly has challenges to tackle, but many people are working to overcome these and see positive signs for the future.

POPULATION

Some estimate that by 2050, India will have a population of approximately 1.53 billion. This is challenging, but it could be worse. Population growth is slowing. In 1950, Indian women averaged six children each. Now the average is slightly less than three. This is largely the result of better health care and education.

CORRUPTION

Another enduring problem in India is corruption and the culture of giving bribes. These include businesses that pay government officials to give them contracts and people who pay public officials to do their jobs properly. During 2001–2010, an estimated $123 billion was taken out of the Indian economy due to corruption. The loss of sums this size slows India's development. An anti-corruption movement organized demonstrations and online protests. In 2012, an anti-corruption political party was established.

THE WAY FORWARD

Indian scientists can play a huge part in making development work. Indian Prime Minister Dr. Manmohan Singh spoke to the Indian Science Congress at the beginning of 2013:

"Faster growth ... more sustainable development based on food and energy security, and socio-economic inclusion made possible by rapid growth of basic social services, such as education and health, are all crucial for defining India's future. Science, technology and innovation all have an important role to play..."

GREEN TECHNOLOGY

While India's development is leading to environmental problems, much is being done to tackle this. Projects include cleaning up the River Ganga to the government's recent commitment to reduce India's greenhouse gas emissions. In 2012, it dedicated over $10 billion to sourcing "green" energy that does not add to greenhouse gases—more than any other major world economy. By doing this, it may help not only India, but the whole world.

A remote road in Himachal Pradesh in northern India. Preserving India's unique environment is one of its biggest challenges for the future.

GLOSSARY

Adivasi tribes of people descended from those who lived in India in prehistoric times; make up approximately 8 percent of the Indian population

agriculture farming

aquifer underground rock that contains water

assassinate to kill someone, usually a public or political figure

Ayurvedic traditional Hindu system of medicine that uses diet, herbal treatment, and breathing exercises

brain drain when skilled and educated people leave a country to work abroad, usually for better opportunities or more money

caste a traditional Indian system of dividing up society; the four main castes are: Brahmin (priests), warriors, traders, and workers.

causeway a raised pathway that crosses water

communications getting information or messages from one place to another, such as sending messages by telephone, computer, or broadcasting

compulsory required by law

corruption being dishonest in business or in government, such as by taking bribes

deforestation clearing away of trees

democracy a form of government in which citizens have a say in the decisions that affect their lives

development the process of growing or advancing, such as a country

moving from traditional forms of agriculture and small-scale industry to more modern forms

dialect a form of a language found in a certain place or among certain people within a nation

diaspora the spread of people away from their country of origin

dowry an amount of money and/or property given by a wife to her husband on marriage

export to sell goods or services to another country

fertilizer a chemical added to soil to make crops grow better

freight goods carried in bulk

GDP (Gross Domestic Product) the value of goods and services a country produces

greenhouse gases gases such as carbon dioxide that are believed to contribute to climate change

green technology energy produced in ways that do not harm the environment, such as using wind, water, or solar (Sun) power to make electricity

heritage sites locations that have special importance due to their beauty or history

hygienic clean; promoting health

import to buy goods or services from another country

Indian National Congress is the oldest Indian political party and has formed most Indian governments since India's independence

inhabitants the people living in a place

invaders armies that enter another country to try to take it over

literacy the ability to read and write

livestock farm animals

middle class people who are not very rich or very poor

migration movement from one place to another

monsoon a major wind system that blows in one direction for a season, and then reverses and blows in the opposite direction.

nepotism when those with power unfairly favor family and friends

peninsula a piece of land that is almost entirely surrounded by water

population density the number of people per unit of area

sacred holy

sitar a stringed musical instrument with a long neck and rounded body

slum an overcrowded area in a town where very poor people live

staple food the foods that people use to make up most of their diet

subcontinent a part of a continent that is almost separate from the rest of it

subsistence farming a type of farming in which most of the crop is consumed by the farmer and only a little is sold for profit

sustainable capable of being maintained without using up natural resources; wind is a sustainable source of energy as it will not run out

sweatshop a factory or workshop, especially in the clothing industry, where people work very long hours for low wages and in poor conditions

tax a payment to the government that is deducted from earnings, sales, or property

telegraph a way of sending messages along a wire by electrical signals

textiles cloth and woven goods, as well as clothing

unpaved a road that has no hard surface

US Civil War a war that occurred in 1861–65 between the northern and southern states of the United States

vaccinating giving an injection of a weak form of a germ carrying a disease to help the body fight off the stronger forms of the disease

West historically describes the countries of Europe and the United States

yoga exercises designed to promore physical and spiritual well being

FURTHER INFORMATION

BOOKS

Countries in our World: India, Darryl Humble (Smart Apple Media, 2010)

DK Eyewitness Travel Guide: India, various authors, (Dorling Kindersley, 2011)

India: People, Place, Culture, History, Philip Wilkinson (Dorling Kindersley, 2008)

WEBSITES

www.cia.gov/library/publications/ the-world-factbook/geos/in.html
Statistics and backround information about India.

www.travel.nationalgeographic. com/travel/countries/india-guide/
Pictures and articles on ancient and modern India, Indian culture, and travel.

www.facts-about-india.com/
Learn about India's history, geography, economy, and more.

www.thefamouspeople.com/ profiles/indira-gandhi-47.php
Learn about Prime Minister Indira Gandhi. She brought about major changes to India's economic, political, international, and national policies.

INDEX